Burning The Night

CW01509369

Burning The Night

Dedicated to an extraordinary soul whose support has guided me not only in poetry, but in life itself. Their insight, honesty, and unwavering presence has been a light along my path. I carry deep gratitude for all they've given me.

Kayliegh
@claryawildepoetry
(Instagram)

Find my poetry on Instagram
@leerogerspoetry

This book is a journey into desire. It begins with the first glance, the spark of attraction that lingers in the air, and moves slowly into the pull of seduction, the tease of restraint, and the tension of surrender. Each stage deepens, building heat until control is lost and passion consumes everything.

But it is not only about fire and frenzy. It is also about worship. The way bodies are adored, the way intimacy can feel like devotion. It is about the softness that follows, the quiet touch, the closeness of skin to skin when the world fades away.

These poems are not simply about lust or love, but about how the two entwine. They explore the moments that take us to the edge of breaking, the tenderness that steadies us, and the hunger that always returns. This is a book of passion in all its forms. Raw, consuming, reverent, and tender.

Part One: Spark

Part Two: Desire

Part Three: Passion

Part Four: Ecstasy

Part Five: Worship

Part Six: Afterglow

Burning The Night

Part One: Spark

The First Glance

your eyes catch mine
across the room—
not long,
not lingering,
but enough
to stop me breathing
and the beat of my heart
quicken for a moment.

there is a weight in it,
a spark i can't name,
and though your gaze moves on,
i feel it still,
burning into me
like a secret
i wasn't meant to see.

i tell myself it was nothing,
but my pulse
doesn't believe it.
i know the truth—
that something began
in that moment,
quiet,
simple,
inevitable.

Pulled Closer

i find you nearer now,
the space between us
smaller than it was before.

your voice drifts through me,
low, steady,
each word carrying
more weight than it should.

i laugh at something small,
but the sound feels fragile,
a cover for the way
your presence presses
against my skin.

your arm brushes mine,
casual, accidental—
yet i swear
the air shifts around us,
charged,
alive.

i don't step away.
i don't want to.
instead i lean closer,
caught in your orbit,
already knowing
that escape
is not what i seek.

The Brush Of Hands

your hand grazes mine,
light, fleeting—
an accident,
or maybe not.

the touch is nothing,
a moment anyone else
would forget—
but it sends a shiver
through my body,
a spark alive
beneath my skin.

i don't look at you,
not right away.
i let the silence hold,
let the question linger
in the space between.

then i feel it again—
your fingers,
closer this time,
not a graze,
but a pause,
a promise.

and suddenly i know:
this is how it begins.
not with a kiss,
not with words,
but with the brush of hands
that changes everything.

The Game Begins

your smile holds mine
a second too long,
a secret folded
behind your lips.

words pass between us,
but it's not the words
that matter—
it's the tone,
the tilt of your head,
the way your eyes linger
just enough to test me.

i answer in kind—
a glance,
a grin,
a silence stretched thin
until it hums.

there is no rush,
only the game—
push, pull,
the line drawn
and crossed again
in the space
between breath and touch.

and i know,
as sure as the fire
beginning to rise,
that neither of us
came here
to play fair.

Drawn Into You

the space between us
shrinks with every breath,
each glance a tether,
each word a thread
pulling me closer.

your laugh curls around me,
warm, low,
like a hand at my back
guiding me forward.

i don't remember
when standing near you
became leaning in—
when leaning in
became reaching out—
only the gravity
of your presence,
how it bends me,
how it keeps me.

your perfume,
your breath,
the brush of your hair
against my arm—
small things
that fill the air
with promise.

and even before
your fingers touch my skin,
i feel you there,
a warmth gathering,
pulling,
a force i no longer
want to resist.

The Promise

your lips hover near,
close enough
to steal my breath,
not close enough
to claim it.

you say nothing—
but your eyes hold me,
a quiet vow
wrapped in silence.

i lean closer,
chasing what you deny,
and you smile,
devilish,
like you've already won.

the air thickens,
every heartbeat
a countdown.
i feel it—
the moment before,
the breaking point,
the promise
of what's to come.

Burning Silence

we stand so close
i can feel your breath
against my cheek—
warm, uneven,
smelling of wine
and wanting.

no words now,
only the hum
that fills the space
between your mouth and mine.

my hand hovers
near your waist,
your fingers curl
like you're about to reach—
but we stay,
suspended,
our bodies speaking
what our voices can't.

every second stretches,
heat gathering
in the pause,
our restraint
its own fire,
burning silently.

Into The Fire

your breath finds mine—
not by accident,
but pulled there,
like a spark leaping
from tinder to flame.

i reach for you,
fingers grazing your waist,
and this time
you don't step back.
you lean in,
closing the last distance
we've been holding.

our lips meet
in a kiss that starts soft,
then deepens—
heat flooding in
where silence was,
a taste of everything
we've been denying.

my hands slip higher,
your body tilts closer,
and the world outside
falls away.
there is only this:
skin and heat,
breath and want,
two bodies
falling together
into the fire.

Part Two: Desire

First Taste

your mouth finds mine—
slow, deliberate,
as though you've waited
a thousand nights
for this moment.

the first brush of lips
isn't gentle—
it's claiming,
a spark leaping skin to skin,
setting me alight.

your tongue
teases the edge of me,
tracing fire
where i've hungered longest,
where restraint
has lived too long.

i fall into you,
every nerve unraveling,
every shiver
a whispered confession
of how much i've ached
to be here.

the kiss deepens,
heat spilling,
breath stolen.
not a question,
not a plea,
but an answer—
the only answer
my body has ever known.

First Touch

your lips hold mine,
but it's your hands
that undo me.

fingers sliding
from jaw to throat,
down to the hollow
where my pulse rages—
a racing beat
calling your name.

you pull me closer,
every inch of distance
burned away.
i am pressed into you,
breath to breath,
skin to skin,
a captive
to our rising heat.

each touch
writes fire
across my body—
a language
only you know,
and only i
can answer.

i cling,
to every sensation,
knowing i am falling—
forever needing
your hands on me.

Exploration

your lips claim mine,
each kiss a promise
that you will take me.
i taste your hunger,
feel it thrum
in the way your mouth
moves against me.
as your hands pull me in
i unravel completely.

your fingers slide
across my skin,
each touch a spark,
each spark
a chain of fire.

your hands roam lower,
mapping me
with restless patience—
the curve of my ribs,
the rise of my chest,
the shiver
when your fingers
dance across my stomach.
you linger,
testing, teasing,
until my breath stumbles,
until my body pleads
without words.

i arch into you,
needing more,
and you answer—
your hands sliding
to the small of my back,
pulling me closer,
pressing heat to heat,
skin to fire.

my gasp
is swallowed by your mouth,
your tongue tasting it,
claiming it,
making it yours.
i am lost
in the rhythm of you—
your lips, your hands,
your breath devouring mine.

the world fades
until nothing exists
but my need for your touch,
only the map you draw
across my body.
i don't care
where the lines lead—
every path
ends in you.

Beneath My Hands

my mouth holds yours,
but it's my hands
that command you—
and you obey.

they drift lower,
slow, deliberate.
i want to feel
every shiver of your body,
every pleading desire
before it escapes.

fingers trace the edges
of forbidden places—
gifts you give to me.
hovering,
teasing,
drawing circles
that make you gasp—
then i pull away,
leaving you trembling,
aching for more.

i see it in your eyes,
i feel it in your skin—
everything i do
is both mercy
and torment,
and you are caught
between begging
and breaking.

Keep You Waiting

your body trembles
beneath my hand,
every muscle
straining toward me,
arching
to reach me.

i hover,
fingers grazing air—
close enough
to make you moan,
yet the simmering heat
between us
is never enough
to satisfy.

you whisper my name,
a plea,
a prayer—
but i smile,
hold you tighter,
and keep you waiting.

because control
is its own pleasure,
and your surrender
is sweetest
when i hear
the wanting
in your voice.

Bound In Need

every nerve aches
from the distance
between us,
straining toward your touch.
the nearness
is torment—
and the air itself
sets me on fire.

i whisper your name,
and your devilish smile,
the hunger in your eyes,
makes me burn
with desperate longing.
and my plea
becomes prayer,
my prayer
becomes begging,
until my voice
is nothing but want.

you hold me in your silence,
bound in restless need,
every second
stretching into forever.
i am undone—
not by your touch,
but by the anticipation
of your hands
on my skin.

The Edge Of Breaking

i am shaking
beneath your gaze,
your eyes spilling heat
across my skin,
my body stretched,
arching,
moving,
on the edge of breaking.

every breath
is filled with you,
every thought
is lost in you,
every second
is fire
building to an inferno
i long for you to quench.

your hand hovers,
teasing,
seducing,
drawing me open
without ever touching.
i arch into nothing,
my voice a cry,
a moan
of sexual aching.

you hold me there—
seduction without touch,
delicious in your power—
until i am nothing
but raw hunger,
stripped of thought,
stripped of will,
stripped of everything
but you.

When Control Breaks

i held you
on a knife-edge
of need—
my smile,
my hovering hands,
my torment, delicious,
carving you open,
until i craved you
as much as you
ached for me.

my breath falters,
my grip tightens,
and you feel it—
the moment
my control
begins to unravel.

you feel it too—
no longer patient,
no longer smiling—
just hungry,
urgent,
my mouth crashes into yours,
claiming.

my hands follow—
every place i teased
now claimed,
pleasured,
set alight.

you shatter
beneath the force of it,
every second of waiting
exploding into release.
and in my arms,
you are nothing
but ruin and rapture,
broken open
and remade
by my hunger.

and i break too,
undone,
consumed
by my need for you.

Burning The Night

Part Three: Passion

Flood

when control breaks,
and patience is lost
between breaths—
only mouths,
only hands,
only the desperate need
to taste,
to claim,
to drown—
consuming us both.

your body yields,
mine devours,
and we fall together
into ruinous pleasure.

skin to skin,
heat to heat,
the world narrowing
to the clash of hips,
the fever of touch,
the reckless tide
of wanting.

every shiver answered
with more fire,
every gasp swallowed
like wine,
every cry met
with the thrust of need
that will not stop.

the sheets twist beneath us,
our bodies slick,
sliding, colliding,
a rhythm fierce,
faster,
until we are nothing
but sound and flame.

there is no time,
no thought,
no silence—
only rhythm,
only moans,
only the flood
sweeping us along
in ravenous passion,
dragging us deeper,
harder,
until we are lost
inside its surge.

Feast

your mouth is on me,
urgent, unyielding,
every kiss a demand,
every taste a claim.

my skin burns
where your lips linger,
my body arching
to meet your hunger.

your hands wander,
reckless, insistent,
pulling me tighter,
pressing me deeper
into your need.

i respond
to every sensation,
no restraint left—
only wild abandon,
flesh to flesh,
hungering lust.

every gasp
becomes offering,
every moan
becomes surrender,
and in your arms
i am devoured—
deliciously,
completely.

and i never
want it to end.

Savour

your mouth slows,
drawing out
every gasp,
every tremor,
every breathless sigh
i give you.

your tongue traces
where fire lingers,
curling, circling,
pausing just enough
to make me shake.
your lips move lower,
then rise again,
mapping me
in a slow, deliberate pattern
that sets every nerve alight.

i can't breathe,
can't think—
my hands clench the sheets,
hips lifting toward you
with each stroke,
with each soft drag
of your mouth.

you murmur against my skin,
heat and breath together,
and the sound vibrates
through me—
a low hum
i feel in my bones.

slow, unyielding,
each touch a reminder
that i am yours—
and i savour it,
the ache and the sweetness,
the way you make my body
open, rise,
shudder under you.

every sigh
another plea you answer,
every moan
a gift you give back,
until the world dissolves
into nothing but the rhythm of you
and the taste of rising ecstasy
you let me hold
a little longer
before it takes me.

Tender Fire

my hands move slower,
a moment of tenderness
amidst the ravenous heat,
feeling
every curve,
every shiver,
every surrendered
truth of you
beneath my touch.

our mouths meet again,
gentle, sensual—
a kiss of reverence,
a kiss of love—
before heat stirs
and the fire
flares between us
once more.

i melt into you,
not with hunger,
but with tenderness—
the way passion softens
when it loves,
the way heat deepens
when it lingers.

Slow Burn

your breath quickens
against my neck,
heat rising
with every kiss
you press into my skin.

your hands tighten,
no longer tender,
but not yet frantic—
fingers tracing fire
that coils low,
that builds slow,
i feel it—
the promise
burning between us.

our bodies shift,
closer,
harder,
heat meeting heat,
and still you hold back—
feeding me the ache
of a slow burn,
drawing me deeper
into the blaze.

Ignite

your hands grip harder,
pulling me closer,
fingers digging just enough
to leave a mark,
our bodies pressed
with no space left
for air or restraint.

every kiss
a spark struck deep,
tongues tangling,
teeth grazing,
each breath shared
like stolen air—
every gasp
fanning the fire
between us.

your hunger rises,
answering mine
with every moan,
every shiver,
every desperate pull,
our hips learning
a harder rhythm,
a faster beat,
a deeper push
that erases thought.

i taste you in my mouth,
feel you in my hands,
the scent of us thick
on our skin—
a fever building
too strong to hold back.

the pace quickens,
the rhythm builds—
we are past holding back,
past slowing down,
sweat slicking our bodies,
heat rolling off us in waves.

the blaze ignites,
filling the room,
filling my lungs,
and there is no
quenching the fire
we've become—
only the rising surge
pulling us closer
to the edge.

Frenzy

the fire surges
between us—
every kiss fierce,
every touch reckless,
our bodies colliding
in a storm
of insatiable desires.

your hands clutch,
mine grasp back,
no tenderness left—
only our frantic passions
to have more,
to give more,
to burn together.

our breaths are ragged,
moans tangled,
the room spinning
with the rhythm of us.

skin slick,
hearts racing,
the world falls away—
there is only fervor,
only fire,
only this frenzy
of our bodies,
and we are lost
in the fire
we've become.

Aftermath

we collapse
into each other,
skin slick,
hearts pounding,
the taste of fire
on our lips,
and streaked
across our skin.

your breath mixes with mine,
ragged, urgent,
as the aching need
to lose ourselves
in ruinous ecstasy
overtakes us completely.

hands roam again,
no pause, no end—
every touch reigniting,
every gasp demanding,
every kiss deeper,
wilder,
until there is no line
between your body and mine.

i feel you everywhere—
in my mouth,
my skin,
my blood—
and still it is not enough.

we break again,
harder,
fiercer,
as ecstatic lust
overwhelms us,
driving us into
rapturous release.

Part Four: Ecstasy

Fire

your body writhes beneath me,
slick with heat,
trembling with the anticipation
of every climax to come—
your eyes pleading
for more.

i give it—
my mouth fierce upon yours,
my hands relentless,
my hips driving us deeper
into the fire we've become.

you gasp my name,
a broken prayer,
and i worship it
with teeth and tongue,
with every thrust
that binds you tighter
to my ruin,
to my rapture.

there is no end,
no pause,
only the holy storm
of bodies colliding,
carnal pleasures
that break us open,
until the night itself
burns for our ecstasy.

Deeper

your legs wrap around me,
pulling me closer,
and i drive into you,
slow at first,
then harder,
my rhythm a demand
your body craves.

your gasp cuts the air—
raw, broken,
yet purring with pleasure
that makes me thrust deeper,
press harder,
chasing the tremor
that ripples through your body.

our mouths crash again,
teeth against lips,
tongues fighting,
devouring—
the kiss as wild
as the heat below.

your fingers clutch,
digging into my skin,
you bite my shoulder—
pain turned to pleasure,
driving me wild.

your voice nothing but moans,
and i lose myself
in the way you writhe,
the way your body begs,
for every thrust.

Driven

the bed shakes with us,
every thrust harder,
every gasp sharper,
the rhythm pounding
like thunder in the dark.

your nails rake my skin,
each mark a command,
each moan a demand
that i answer
with hips,
with teeth,
with fire.

sweat runs between us,
slick and burning,
our bodies slipping,
sliding,
colliding again—
need against need,
heat against heat.

we are nothing
but sound and motion,
a fever of animalistic instinct,
and i drive into you
harder,
faster,
the fire itself
taking hold of me.

Consumed

every inch of you
takes me deeper—
skin, scent,
the wet slick press
of flesh against flesh.
i bury my face
in the hollow of your neck,
taste the pulse there,
and it pulls me into its beat.

you arch,
you call my name,
a sound ripped
from some low place—
and i answer with more:
hands that travel,
fingers that find secret places,
pushing you to the edge,
each tense pulse
pounding through your body.

our pace becomes urgent—
no hesitation,
only the heat of the animal rhythm.
we grind and press,
we buck and hold,
our bodies learning
how to break and bind,
the bed a canvas beneath us,
painted in release.

your breath shreds into mine,
a ragged hymn;
i drink it down,
feed it back with harder thrusts,
each motion carving you deeper into me.

there is no mercy here—
only the sweet abandon of wanting,
only the endless fall
into taking and giving,
until the edges blur,
and we find ourselves swallowed
by the very thing we made.

Tremor

the pressure mounts
beneath my palm,
small movements
that mean so much—
a hip that shifts an inch,
a clench, a soft plea,
and the world narrows
so all that exists
is you and i.

your skin trembles under me,
an electric shiver of need—
i trace it with deliberate force,
thumbs pressing, knuckles brushing,
fingers finding the places
that make you buckle.

each brush is a promise,
each slide a test:
how close can i drive you
before you break?
how much can you take
and still beg for more?

you answer in half-moans,
in caught breaths,
in the way your thighs tighten—
and it makes me harder,
more precise, more certain.

there is a sweetness here—
a near-reckless patience,
hands that tempt,
touches that tease.

the tremor builds—
a last taut breath
before we descend
into ravenous fire.

Feral Heat

you drag your mouth across me,
not gentle, not patient—
every kiss a bruise,
every bite a claim.

my name rips from you,
half-moan, half-snarl,
and i answer with teeth,
tongue,
fingers digging hard enough
to leave marks you'll wear for days.

our bodies grind together,
slick, relentless,
chasing friction,
chasing fire.
every thrust rougher,
every gasp torn,
the rhythm breaks into chaos—
and it only makes us hungrier.

your nails score my back,
my hand fists in your hair,
we pull, claw, devour—
each second hotter,
harder,
rawer.

there is no pause,
no tenderness,
only the ravenous sweetness
of need unbound,
rising, raging,
driving us both
closer to ruin.

Untethered

restraint is a lost memory—
hands no longer gentle,
voices gone hoarse,
a rough chorus of need
that drowns the world.

you pull me,
i pull back,
we fall together,
no rhythm
but the one we make—
faster,
harder,
wilder.

every touch is a demand,
every kiss a seizure,
tongues and teeth
and breath colliding,
each motion a bright,
burning untethered release.

my skin is a map of your want—
marks,
prints,
the architecture of need—
and i answer in kind,
in nails and moans,
in everything raw and unrefined.

there is no careful slow now—
only the surge,
the panic-hunger
that loves uncontrolled,
the way our bodies slam
and break and call—
breathless,
frantic,
deliciously undone.

you howl,
i howl back—
two wild things,
uncomposed,
unmade,
ecstatic in the ruin,
and still it climbs,
higher,
harsher,
hungrier—
the final snap waiting
just beyond the next thrust.

First Climax

the snap comes sudden—
a scream, a shudder,
your body convulsing around me,
dragging me with you
into the climax.

i thrust once more,
harder,
harder—
and our world explodes.

pleasure tears me open,
white-hot,
blinding—
every nerve unraveling,
every vein set alight.

you claw my back,
i cry out,
our voices jagged thunder,
our bodies thrashing,
breaking apart,
breaking open—
until nothing exists
but fire.

we spill together,
uncontrolled,
endless,
collapsing into ruin,
skin slick, hearts erratic,
the world erased
in rapture's flood.

and in that ruin,
something stirs—
a silence of spent bodies,
breath heavy and soft,
a new heat rising.

Part Five: Worship

Embers

we lie broken,
skin glistening with sweat,
hearts still pounding
from the storm we made.

the air is thick with us—
the scent of sex,
still lingering in the dark,
and the echo of fire
that has not yet died.

your chest rises,
falls,
each breath a shiver
against my skin.
my hands linger,
soft now,
tracing the ruin we became,
finding beauty
in every mark
we left behind.

i kiss your shoulder,
your throat,
not with hunger,
not relentless fervour
but reverence—
each touch a vow
that the worship has only begun,
that this silence
is not the end,
but the promise
of more.

Devotion

my hands move like ritual,
learning every curve,
every hollow,
tracing the map
your skin became
as i worship your body.

i press my mouth to places
with delicate reverence—
a collarbone,
the soft hollow
below your throat,
the small curve
at the back of your knee—
and you answer with a murmur
at each press of my lips.

my fingers make no demand;
they only give.
lips slow and certain,
tongue worshipful,
attentive—
i taste you as one tastes prayer,
small, reverent sips
that build into an offering.

you lift your face to me,
eyes hooded;
i read confession in your breath—
the way your hands find my hair,
the tilt of your hips,
asking, asking—
and i oblige with complete devotion:
patient, exact—
my single need:
to satiate your every desire.

Consecration

you move with intent—
each touch feeds an ember
that burns and widens inside me;
each kiss an answered vow.

you find the places
that make me forget names—
the hollow at my throat,
the soft curve beside my ribs—
places where sound
blooms into light.

my body yields,
answering as you pour yourself into worship—
you do not take;
you give and lavish,
mouth and hands learning scripture:
fingers that press the right chord,
tongue that teases the chord that makes me fall.
your whole world narrows
to the tremor of my skin,
and every moan
becomes sacrament.

we do not rush to ruin;
we consecrate—
no haste in this chamber,
only slow pilgrimage
from secret to secret,
mouth to hollow,
hand to fold—
until my sighs are altars,
and my cries
the only scripture
you need to read.

i fold around release,
quiet, sacred, steady—
you hold me through the spill,
gently, insistently—
so what is to come is not merely spent
but offered, sanctified:
a second rise,
fuller,
hungrier—
because worship has taught us
the art of waiting,
and the way to drown in pleasure.

Offering

your body glows beneath my hands,
each curve a sacred oasis
i have only begun to explore.
i linger over every rise,
every fall,
as though to memorize each form
into my flesh.

my lips follow,
soft at first—
a kiss at the curve of your hip,
a slow taste of your skin,
and i feel you shiver
in the ache of wanting,
in the ache of waiting.

you tilt toward me,
a silent plea,
and i answer in part—
my mouth grazing,
my tongue tasting,
never fully,
not yet.

the gift is in the delay,
in the slow gathering of want.
and so i give not the storm,
but the anticipation—
the reverent touch
that leaves you trembling,
certain the flood will come.

Threshold

i move with the care
of someone nurturing a flame,
hands steady, breath measured—
learning how close i can come
before the heat
demands everything from me.

your skin answers under my palm,
a storm kept small,
a pulse racing beneath silk.
i trace the edge of your want,
lighter and nearer with each pass,
feeling the way your breath hitches—
a tiny quake that maps the line
between patience and surrender.

my kisses grow hungrier,
not frantic, not urgent—
pressing,
seeking,
tasting places
that make your back arch
and your voice thin.
i place my mouth where desire lives most,
and you fold toward me,
inch by trembling inch.

the silence between our breaths grows thick—
a charged space
where restraint ends
and pull begins.
you press back,
testing,
asking,
and i give enough to feed the need,
but never the flood—
because worship here is also craft:
to know the exact moment
to lean in,
and the exact moment
to hold.

your fingers find me then—
urgent, pleading—
and the restraint we practiced unravels a thread.
the tremor builds
beneath our skin,
a promise felt in the bones,
and we stand—
on the verge,
the threshold, exhaled in every breath.

Supplication

your body opens beneath me,
every sigh a command,
every tremor a prayer i obey.
my mouth moves lower,
my hands sliding across your skin—
every touch a delicate control,
keeping you from unraveling
too soon.

i worship you with hunger again,
tongue circling, lips pulling,
each motion designed
to draw another cry,
another wave,
until your voice becomes a litany
of broken pleasure.

you writhe,
you sigh,
you moan,
your thighs tighten around me,
and i stay, unrelenting,
drinking in every sound you give,
tasting each release
your body spills.

this is worship in its purest form—
not prayer spoken to the heavens,
but prayer answered here,
in flesh, in heat,
in the way you break open
under my devoted worship.

Ecstasy Of Worship

your voice is a hymn,
rising with every gasp,
and i press deeper
into the altar of your body.

my tongue learns your rhythm,
your sighs guiding me closer,
each tremor a sermon
feeding my devotion.

my hands anchor you—
every movement caught
in the wave that builds,
that sacred quake
running through your frame.

i drink you in,
unyielding, relentless,
each taste a vow,
each moan a scripture.
your body arches,
your fingers tangle in my hair,
pulling me harder,
pleading without words,
and i answer in devotion,
in worship,
in fire.

you open wider,
a trembling surrender,
and i pour myself into you—
lips, tongue, breath,
every part of me praising,
adoring,
consuming—
until the air itself is thick
with holy desire.

and when you cry out,
it is not ruin—
it is revelation.

Sanctified

the wave rises,
a tide drawn by prayer
and pulled by devotion.

your voice breaks—
not words,
but pure sound,
a cry that trembles
in rising climax.

my mouth does not relent;
i hold you steady,
each motion deliberate,
each stroke a vow fulfilled.
your thighs close around me,
pulling me nearer—
closer, deeper,
until all you are
is release waiting to fall.

and then it comes—
your body shudders,
your back arches,
your breath collapses.
a sacred quake
that tears you open
and pours through me too.

i drink the moment whole,
and you are radiant—
spent yet burning,
broken yet holy,
trembling in the quiet flood
of rapture's gift.

the room is silence after thunder,
the air thick with reverence.
your body glistens,
our hearts beat as one,
and in my worship
you are remade—
not undone,
but sanctified.

Part Six: Afterglow

After The Fire

the world feels quieter now,
but you still burn in me—
not as worship,
not as prayer,
but as flesh and heat
and the simple truth
that i cannot let you go.

your breath lingers on my skin,
every sigh a ghost of what we were
minutes before,
and my hands
cannot stop tracing
the memory of you.

i do not think of sanctity—
i think of sweat,
and teeth,
and the way you moaned my name
like it was the only thing
that kept you alive.

i hold you close,
not as altar,
but as lover—
because after the fire,
what i want most
isn't worship,
but more of you.

Skin To Skin

your head rests against my chest,
breath warm on my skin,
and i trace circles
along your back
just to feel you breathe.

the room is quiet now,
our bodies cooling but still damp,
a glow where heat was,
a pulse where fire burned.

i run my fingers
over the curve of your hip,
down your thigh,
my gaze following
as i take in the beauty
of your body.

you shift,
half-asleep,
half-smiling,
and i press a delicate kiss
to your hairline,
my lips a whisper
against your skin.

we do not speak.
we do not need to.
this is enough—
skin to skin,
heartbeat to heartbeat,
our bodies spent,
our hearts still trembling
in the embers of the fire we made.

The Quiet Between Us

your fingers find mine
without searching,
our hands fitting together
fingers lacing
as if they were always
destined to fit
so perfectly.

the room holds its breath,
a hush so complete
i can almost hear
the beat of your heart,
and the small sigh
you don't know you're making.

we stay like this—
no words,
no movement,
your head against my shoulder,
my thumb tracing
slow circles
on the back of your hand.

i watch your lashes tremble,
feel the flutter of breath
against my collarbone,
the weight of you
settling into me
like you were always meant to.

there is nothing to do
but be here,
skin and warmth,
our hearts beating as one,
the quiet between us
as full
as everything
we've already given.

Tracing You

my fingers wander
with a slow savour,
following every line
of your body—
collarbone to shoulder,
spine to hip—
memorising you
in gentle strokes.

your skin warms beneath my touch,
a quiet hum
that rises each time
my palm slides
a little lower.
i press my mouth to you
in small, careful kisses,
each one
still alight with a spark
of fire we made.

you shift against me,
breath catching,
your hand finding mine
to guide it
where you want me most.
but i linger,
draw circles instead,
tracing you
inch by inch,
letting the wanting
build slow between us.

our bodies stay close,
not frantic—
just this low, tender burn
gathering under our skin,
two hearts beating steady,
fingers and lips
teaching each other again
how to begin.

You In My Arms

i hold you close,
the warmth of our skin
a sensation
i want to last,
hearts pressed
into the same rhythm.

your breath drifts over me,
soft, steady,
and i breathe it in
like air i cannot live without.

my arms curl tighter—
the need to have you near,
to keep you wrapped
inside the circle of me.

you murmur something low,
half-word, half-sigh,
and i answer
with lips at your temple,
a kiss without urgency,
just the quiet truth
that i cannot stop
loving you
in this moment.

the world fades.
all that matters
is this—
you in my arms,
me in yours,
the kind of closeness
that feels endless.

Soft Fire

your touch lingers,
slow as embers,
trailing warmth
across my skin.

it is not hunger,
but something gentler—
a quiet flame
that asks to be fed.

my hand finds yours,
guides it higher,
lower,
until breath stirs
between us again,
until silence breaks
with the catch
in my throat.

your lips brush mine,
unhurried,
but the spark leaps—
a kiss that deepens
with every second,
heat pressing back
into the space
between our bodies.

there is no rush,
no frenzy,
only the low burn
of wanting returning—
a soft fire
gathering strength,
ready to rise.

Slow Rising

your breath quickens
against my mouth,
a soft sound
that stirs something deeper.

our kiss lingers—
still gentle,
but heavier now,
a promise pressed
between parted lips.

my hands begin to wander,
not in haste,
but in need—
palms learning again
the fire waiting
beneath your skin.

you arch into me,
a sigh escaping,
and i feel the shift—
the tremor
when tenderness
tips into hunger.

we do not rush;
we let it build,
heat gathering
in patient waves,
each touch
another spark
feeding the slow rising blaze.

Unfinished

your hands slide beneath me,
no more hesitation,
no more quiet—
fingers tracing fire
until my breath falters
and the ache rushes back,
full and certain.

our mouths collide,
kisses no longer gentle,
teeth, tongue, breath—
a hunger returning
like a tide
we cannot hold back.

heat builds fast,
spilling from touch
into motion,
our bodies finding
that urgent rhythm
we've been holding at bay.

i press closer,
you pull harder,
each sound a spark
until the room flickers
with our low moans,
our broken gasps,
the taste of want
becoming heat,
becoming fire again.

we rise together,
the afterglow gone,
the soft burn transformed—
and at the very edge
of another beginning
we pause,
breathless,
shaking,
unfinished.

Printed in Dunstable, United Kingdom

72259364R00067